THE PENGUIN
AND THE PEA

To Judith

A thousand peas and thank yous to editor Debbie Rogosin and the people at
Kids Can Press for their encouragement and skillful guidance.

Text and illustrations © 2004 Janet Perlman
Based on *The Princess and the Pea*, by Hans Christian Andersen.

Kids Can Press acknowledges the financial support of the Government of Ontario, through the Ontario Media
Development Corporation's Ontario Book Initiative; the Ontario Arts Council; the Canada Council for the Arts; and the
Government of Canada, through the BPIDP, for our publishing activity.

Published in Canada by
Kids Can Press Ltd.
29 Birch Avenue
Toronto, ON M4V 1E2

Published in the U.S. by
Kids Can Press Ltd.
2250 Military Road
Tonawanda, NY 14150

www.kidscanpress.com

The artwork in this book was drawn in ink on paper and then colored in Photoshop.
The text is set in Kennerly.

Edited by Debbie Rogosin
Designed by Karen Powers and Kathleen Collett
Printed and bound in Hong Kong, China, by Book Art Inc., Toronto

This book is smyth sewn casebound.

CM 04 0 9 8 7 6 5 4 3 2 1

National Library of Canada Cataloguing in Publication Data

Perlman, Janet, (date)
The penguin and the pea / retold and illustrated by Janet Perlman.

ISBN 1-55074-832-7

I. Title.

PS8581.E726P45 2004   jC813'.54   C2003-905709-7

Kids Can Press is a *corus*™ Entertainment company

THE PENGUIN
AND THE PEA

RETOLD AND ILLUSTRATED BY
JANET PERLMAN

Kids Can Press

L ong ago in a faraway land, there lived a Penguin Prince
who was very very lonely. He wished more than anything
to find a penguin princess to marry, but she had to be a
real princess.

He traveled far and wide to find one, and he met many
penguins who claimed to be princesses. Some even wore crowns.
But there was always something that was not quite right.

One was too loud; another, too giddy; this one too shy; that one just plain boring.

The Prince was not impressed by any of them, and so he returned home, weary and discouraged.

"I fear I will never find the penguin princess of my dreams!"
he lamented.

His parents, too, had hopes of seeing their son marry a true
princess, and their hearts ached to see him so unhappy.

One night there was a terrible storm. Lightning flashed on the castle walls, and the wind howled through the trees. The rain came down in torrents, flooding the courtyard.

Suddenly, there was a loud banging at the castle gate. Who could be out on such a night? The old King himself went to see.

Outside the gate stood a wet and miserable penguin. Her carriage had broken down, and she was seeking shelter from the storm.

She claimed to be a princess — but what a dreadful sight she was! Rain streamed from her beak, and her feathers were all matted. Her clothes were in tatters, and her crown was caked with mud. Yet she insisted that she was a real princess.

The King invited the shivering penguin in to dry off
and stay for the night.

The Princess shook the rain and mud from her clothes
and feathers as best she could. When she removed her
grubby rainflippers, enough water gushed out to make a
puddle in the entranceway.

The old Queen pursed her beak disapprovingly at their
bedraggled guest.

"She does not look like a princess to me!" she said to the
King. "Just look at those scraggly feathers! That rusty crown!"

But the Prince was intrigued by the mysterious stranger,
and looked forward to learning more about her.

As the evening wore on, he saw that despite everyone's first impression, she possessed genuine beauty and a sparkling wit. In all his travels he had never met anyone as enchanting as she. From the gentle curve of her beak down to her delicately webbed feet, she was the most perfect penguin princess he had ever seen!

As for the Princess, she had never before met so handsome and charming a prince.

The Queen could see that her son was captivated, but she was very suspicious of the Princess. Thinking she was an impostor who was only after her handsome son, the Queen hatched a plan to make sure their guest would not stay long.

While the Princess was warming her feathers in front of the fire, the Queen went into one of the guest chambers and had the servants remove all the bedding. She then placed a large firm green cabbage on the bed, and over it a flimsy threadbare mattress.

"Our so-called princess will be gone by the crack of dawn after sleeping on this bed!" chortled the Queen.

When it came time to retire for the night, the Princess
was shown to her bedchamber.

"Oh dear, this certainly is a lumpy old bed!" she thought.

She tried her best to get comfortable, but all through the
night she flipped and flopped and did not sleep a wink.

The next morning she said not a word about her terrible night. Like most princesses, she was too polite to complain, although everyone could see that she was exhausted. The Queen thought regretfully that the Princess was now too tired to travel. The storm was still raging, and the Princess was happy to stay at the castle and spend more time with the Prince.

It was a day of pure delight and whimsy. The two young penguins talked about everything and anything. They were simply enchanted with each other, and the castle halls rung with joy and laughter.

"She surely must be a real princess," thought the Prince. "She is the ideal penguin for me."

By the end of the day the Prince was so in love that he asked
for her fin in marriage. The Princess happily accepted.

The Prince then went to his parents to ask for their blessing.
The King gave his flap of approval right away, for he could see
how much in love his son was.

But the Queen was not ready to welcome the newcomer into the royal family.

"We must be absolutely sure that this young penguin is a real princess!" the Queen insisted. "Only a true princess is so delicate and fragile as to feel a single pea under twenty mattresses. If she passes this test, then you will have my blessing."

Now the Queen was not absolutely certain that this was a precise test of being a real princess, but it was the only one she knew. Anyone could feel a cabbage under a mattress — but a pea ...

She hurried back to the guest chamber, removed the cabbage and put in its place one tiny green pea.

She then ordered the servants to bring nineteen more mattresses to be placed on top. Finally, just to be sure, she ordered twenty heavy eiderdown quilts to be added to the pile.

When the Princess entered the bedchamber and saw
the towering bed, she was bewildered.

"Could this be the same bed I slept on last night? It
looks very different!"

But all her things were there, just as she had left them,
so it had to be the right room.

The Princess had quite a time climbing up onto the bed.
When she finally reached the top, the height made her
extremely dizzy. And then, once she was nestled in, she
could feel something hard beneath the mattresses that was
causing her some discomfort.

In the middle of the night, as she turned restlessly from side to side, she rolled right off the bed and tumbled to the floor!

She sat up and carefully adjusted her crown. Her whole body ached, her flippers were bruised and some of her feathers were broken. She did not even try to climb back up, but huddled miserably on the floor for the rest of the night.

In the morning when the Princess came down to the royal
breakfast table, the Queen asked, "How did you sleep last night,
my dear? I do hope the bed was comfortable." The Princess was
not sure what to say, for she did not want to complain.

"Don't be shy. Please tell us," the Queen urged. Everyone
leaned closer to hear her reply.

"Oh, it was a lovely bed. So many mattresses and quilts," the Princess began. "But there was something hard in it that kept me awake all night! And then ... oh I cannot tell you how I have suffered! I am covered in bruises and I'm sore all over!"

"I knew she was a real princess!" exclaimed the Prince.
How happy he was!

From then on the Princess was recognized by everyone in
the kingdom to be genuine royalty, for she had felt a tiny pea
right through twenty mattresses and twenty eiderdown quilts.

The Queen gave her consent, and the Prince and Princess
were soon married and lived flappily ever after.

As for the pea, it was put on display in a special
glass case in the Royal Penguin Museum. It remains
there to this day — if it hasn't been lost.
And so ends a true story.